W9-CGQ-934

A Day So GRAY

by Marie Lamba

art by Alea Marley

Clarion Books
Houghton Mifflin Harcourt
Boston New York

Clarion Books
3 Park Avenue
New York, New York 10016

Clarion Books is an imprint of Houghton Mifflin Harcourt Publishing Company.

hmhbooks.com

The illustrations in this book were done using
scanned scribbly textures, Photoshop, and a touch of magic.
The text was set in Doug.
Hand-lettering by Mike Burroughs

Library of Congress Cataloging-in-Publication Data

Names: Lamba, Marie, author. | Marley, Alea, illustrator.
Title: A day so gray / by Marie Lamba ; illustrated by Alea Marley.
Description: Boston ; New York : Clarion Books, Houghton Mifflin Harcourt, [2019] | Summary: "A winter's day is transformed from bleak to beautiful by warm friendship and a new perspective in a gentle story that encourages the appreciation and celebration of cozy pleasures and quiet joys"-- Provided by publisher.
Identifiers: LCCN 2018051998 | ISBN 9781328695994 (hardcover picture book)
Subjects: | CYAC: Color--Fiction. | Winter--Fiction. | Friendship--Fiction.
Classification: LCC PZ7.L1676 Day 2019 | DDC [E]--dc23
LC record available at https://lccn.loc.gov/2018051998

Manufactured in China
SCP 10 9 8 7 6 5 4 3 2 1
4500768035

To my father, Santo Busterna, who taught me
there is beauty and color in every landscape
—M.L.

To my mother and father, who always helped me
through days that only felt gray
—A.M.

This day
is so gray.
No, it isn't! . . .

It's deep soft brown,
and shining blue,
and silver splashes
on bright yellow.

This field is
blah brown.

No, it isn't! . . .

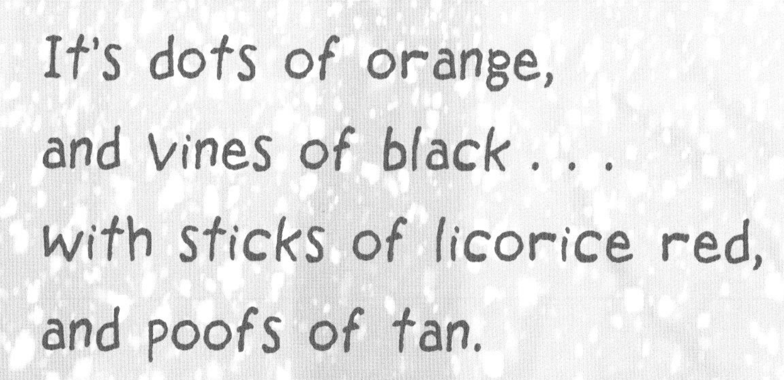

It's dots of orange,
and vines of black . . .
with sticks of licorice red,
and poofs of tan.

Well, this snow
is boring white.

No, it isn't! . . .

It's lines of purple,
and squiggles of gray.
It's gems of twinkling silver,
with stomps of green.

Bad luck!
That cat
is black!
She's not
all black! . . .

She's also soft pads of pink,
and specks of white.

And eyes glowing yellow-green.

Plus she's warm, and that's a good thing.

So is
this fire.
The fire is orange.
I don't like orange.

It isn't just orange.
It's flashes of red
and yellow.

And sizzling black logs,
and gray bits of smoke.

Well,
it is cozy.

Yes.
Yes, it is.

And so is the blue, green, red blanket.
And so is the black, pink, white cat.

And so is the brown,
white, gray
cocoa.

And so is the
purple and
tangerine
sunset.

And we are cozy, too,
on this day
that was so much
more than gray!